DON'T LET GO!

ÉLISABETH EUDES-PASCAL

OWLKIDS BOOKS

Last one in is a rotten egg!

Let's jump in!
No!

I want you to hold me!

Batter up!
And don't let go!

Do you want the donut?

Home run!
I want the donut!

Hee hee hee!
Ouch!

Why don't you float on your own?
I want you to hold me!
Look, I'm a seal!

Hello!
And don't let go!
Do you want the flutterboard?

I want the flutterboard!

Hee hee hee!
Ouch!

Why don't you float on your own?
I had it first!
Dad!

No, I want you to hold me!

And don't let go...

...I want the noodle!

Ugh! It's warm!
Hee hee hee!
Ouch!

Why don't you float on your own?
Hello?

Look, Mom! A fish!
No, I want you to hold me!

Do you want to play with the ball?
And don't let go!
There's one!
I don't see it!

I want the ball!

Burp!
Ouch!
Hee hee hee!
Say cheese!

Got one!
One, two, three!
Dive with us,
Mom!

Look, Dad! A boat!
The ice is melting!

Do you see the boat?
Yes! What a nice boat!
And see how it floats!
Just like you!

Can I get my ball back?

I want Mommy to hold me!